HODI'S
KILIMANJARO ADVENTURES

by K. Alana Jones

Illustrations by Blueberry Illustrations

Boutique Publishing

Washington, D.C.

Published by Boutique Publishing Company
P.O. Box 5485
Washington, DC 20016

ISBN-10: 069202770X
ISBN-13: 978-0-692-02770-7

It's almost sunset. It's the time of day when the sun is getting sleepy. Mother Lion called for Hodi to wake up. She called louder.

"Yes, I'm up," Hodi responded, stretching. She laid down again.

"Wake up daughter. It will be dusk soon. We have work to do. We have to go hunting for our supper."

Hodi complained, "It's too hot. What happened to all the prey we brought home yesterday?"

"We ate it," Mother replied.

Hodi does not like hunting because she is no good at it. She would rather be playing or sleeping.

"Don't be a sack of lazy bones. Come on. Let's go now," Mother Lion said as she dashed out of the den and into the meadow.

Hodi followed far behind. On the way, they came to the cave where their cousin Mimi Leopard lives. Now, Mimi Leopard never allows her daughter, Juma, to play with Hodi because she thinks she's a goof-off.

"Hello Mimi," Mother Lion waved.

"Oh hi," she responded. "You're going hunting I see. My Juma is already out hunting for the first time on her own," she bragged. "How ever did you get her out of the lazy sack?" Mimi laughed.

Mother Lion did not answer. "We'll be on our way. See you around. Let's go, Hodi."

"I don't know why you're so nice to her," Hodi shook her head.

"In this case, she's right. You have to start working harder. If you're not passionate about hunting, then you have got to have passion about something one day."

Mother lion and Hodi joined the other lionesses that had all come together to hunt for dinner. There in the meadow were a herd of zebra that looked, oh, SO yummy. Everyone took their positions. They licked their whiskers, quietly approached, then - CHARGE!!

It was the perfect chase. Hodi could see everything from behind the perfect rock she found sitting behind a perfect tree. On the way home, Hodi began playing chase with a beautiful butterfly after it landed on her nose. It flew into the forest and she chased it. Mother called, "Don't stay away too long and come directly home." She continued walking home with the other lionesses.

Hodi was thirsty so she ran to a waterfall to quench her thirst. Just as she began to take a drink, she heard rustling in the trees and became nervous. She looked up and then down. She looked all around. She felt a tap on her shoulder and .....

"EEEkkk!!"

Oh, what a relief! It was just cousin Juma?

"What are you doing in the trees, Juma? I thought...," Hodi became suspicious. "I thought you were supposed to be hunting."

"I am," Juma responded.

"You're hunting from up there in the trees?"

"No, I mean I am supposed to be hunting but I'm afraid so I'm hiding."

"Well, what will you tell your mother when she expects you to bring home meat?"

"I don't know yet," Juma said sadly.

"You have to tell her that you're scared," Hodi advised.

"No way! She'll be so disappointed in me. She always tells me to be brave," Juma hung her head. "I just wish she didn't brag about me so much. It's hard for me to do anything right when she expects so much of me. I dare not embarrass her."

"What are you going to do?" Hodi asked.

"I can't go back now. I can't face her disappointment, again. I think I need to talk to our friend Uhuru."

Hodi and Juma walked to the other side of the grassland just at the opening of the tropical forest where many animals and insects call their home.

They lifted up the rock where their friend, Uhuru the spider, lives. They distracted him and all of his dinner ran away.

"Ohhhh!!!" Uhuru was desparate.

"We're sorry, Uhuru."

"Didn't your mother ever teach you to knock?"

Hodi scratched her head, "No."

"Well, what are you two doing here anyway?"

Juma answered, "Um, well, I was trying to hunt, but it's no use. I'll never be any good at it. Hodi's not very good at it either."

Uhuru took a break from searching. "Don't worry. You'll make your mother proud one day. You just keep being yourself."

Juma was encouraged. "Maybe one day Hodi and I will do something great together."

"That's the attitude," Uhuru said while gathering whatever he could salvage from his runaway dinner.

After cheering up, they all played fun games in the heat while the sun was still shining. The heat was too much for Hodi.

Hodi asked, "Uhuru, was it as hot in your homeland as it is here?"

"Oh yes but hotter!" he replied. "One day I'll go back there but right now I don't want to think about it."

They played and played some more.

Hodi and Juma wrestled a little too close to the edge of a cliff and Hodi tumbled over.

They ran down to help her. Hodi stood up to dust herself off. While holding her head to regain her senses, she looked out to the sky. There, off in the distance was the most fascinating sight. Her mouth dropped in awe and her eyes danced with wonder.

"What is that?" Hodi asked.

"What's what?" Juma and Uhuru asked.

"That!" Hodi exclaimed.

"Oh, that? It's nothing. I see it all the time." Juma pretended to know the answer. "It's one of those, those fluffy things," she said while pointing to the clouds.

As Hodi stared in amazement, Uhuru became worried that she was getting some ideas in her head.

"It's a mountain with snow on top. It's so far away from here," he warned.

"I have to go to that mountain. I wonder if it is as hot there as it is here. I wonder if there are other lions there. I just want to touch it."

"No, it's such a long way," Uhuru said. You're not able to survive such a long trip. First, it rains. Then, it gets even hotter, and then, it becomes too cold for a lion to survive. Here, every day is the same."

"Yeh, hot and boring." Hodi complained. "All day long I sleep under trees, watch my family hunt and eat."

"You just don't understand the dangers." Uhuru could not believe his ears.

Hodi would not listen. "Juma are you going with me?"

"Uh uh, no way. I'm already standing on a mountain of trouble," Juma refused.

"Then I have to go tell my father and mother that I'm going on a journey that could make me the most important lion in the grassland. Maybe then they will see that I'm not just a hunter. I'm an adventurer," Hodi proclaimed.

Hodi and Juma ran as fast as they could toward home. When they arrived home, daylight was gone. There were Mimi Leopard and Mother Lion pacing around waiting and worrying. "What were you thinking going off and staying away for so long? You scared us and you should be ashamed. Your father is so angry. He's gone out looking for the two of you," Mother Lion scolded.

"I'm sorry that I'm late mother. I have something to tell you that will make you so proud of me," Hodi announced. She was so excited but Mother Lion was not hearing any of it. "I, I have decided to go on a journey to discover a mountain."

Mimi Leopard shrieked with laughter.

Mother said, "How is that supposed to make us proud? You're running away? Humph!"

"I'm not running away. I'll be right back don't worry."
She convinced her mother to let her go on the journey.

There was no stopping her. Mother packed for her a satchel of meat. Hodi kissed them all good-bye and left. She ran and ran and ran. She ran deep into the deep, dark tropical rain forest when......

"Why   you   so

are   running   fast?" she heard a voice cry.

"Huh?!" Hodi stopped suddenly to look down in her pocket.

"Quit running. You want me to lose yesterday's dinner too?" Uhuru said poking his head out of Hodi's pocket.

Hodi was confused. "What are you doing in there?"

Uhuru had some explaining to do. "I just thought maybe you would need someone to protect you from wild animals."

"Uhuru, I'm a lion. I'm as wild as they come."

"Oh yeah – well, uh, you know," Uhuru sighed. "I, I was hoping you would take me to my homeland."

"I see – no problem. I could use the company anyway."

Hodi plopped down in exhaustion. They walked to find a nice place to rest for the night and found a soft pile of leaves to rest until morning.

"SSSSsssss," said Ferny the
Snake.

"SSSSsssss," said Lucy the
Snake.

"She must be lost. She's asleep.
Let's bite her," Ferny suggested.

"Whoa. She's a lion ya know and we
don't want any trouble," Lucy was
hesitant.

This shocked Ferny. He said,
"You look like a snake but you
sound like a chicken. Stay here,
then. Bragging rights are coming right up."

Lucy shook her head in disgust and
mumbled, "This is going to be good."

Ferny crept over to the tree that hung above Hodi and
slid down to strike. Just then, Hodi opened her eyes
and saw Ferny. She jumped to her feet. Poor Uhuru
was sleeping on Hodi's paw and went flying into the air.
Hodi roared at the snake right before it scurried back
into the trees and out of sight.

Uhuru went soaring back down to the ground but Hodi caught him before he hit. They were both relieved. Then –

"SSSSsssss!!!" Lucy hissed from behind to finish the job and Hodi took off running through the trees.

"I have to do everything around here," Lucy complained.

They ran and ran until before they knew it they were running out of the forest and up a steep, dry hill.

"Huff, puff. Hey! We made it out," panted Hodi. "And look, it's even closer now!" pointing to the mountain.

"Well then, let's get moving," Uhuru suggested.

But then, something else caught Hodi's eye. "Hey, look down there on that side of the hill. It looks just like my home."

Hodi noticed a place where the grass was even taller than home and there were elephants and a river as far as she could see. She leaped with excitement.

"Let's go there," Hodi suggested.

Uhuru was skeptical about things working out smoothly.

Hodi headed down to the river. "Oh, just for a minute. I want to go and get a drink of water."

They heard an angry voice from behind. "Hey!! Where do you think you're going?"

Hodi saw behind her two very mean looking lions.

"This is our territory and don't go thinking we need any help around here from you."

"Well, I just wanted a drink of water. I'm on my way to...."

"*ROAR!!* Maybe you don't hear so well so enough talking!"

As the lions walked toward Hodi, she walked backwards.

Uhuru yelled from her pocket, "Run, Hodi!"

She took off running back up the hill but the lions caught her and tackled her to the ground. The two lions snatched the satchel of food that she was carrying. "This stays here. Now beat it loser. *GGGRRR!!!*"

She ran frantically up and over the hill. She ran and ran until she came to open land that was so dry where the sun beamed so brightly.

She stopped to catch her breath.

"Hey!" Uhuru gasped. This is my home. We've have made it! Over there is where I last saw my family before I was carried off," he pointed to a shrub. He noticed that Hodi was not as enthusiastic as he was. He felt bad for her. "Hodi, I'm sorry about your satchel."

She was worried. "What will I eat now?"

Uhuru wanted to cheer her up. "There are plenty of desert birds around here."

Hodi felt lonely. "Will I ever make it back to see my mom and dad again? We're so far away now. When you find your family, I'll be all alone. This was a big mistake."

"No. You're going to be somebody. You'll see. Sure, you're going about it the hard way, but it'll pay off."

"Do you think so?" Hodi wiped her tears and patted Uhuru with a smile. "Let's keep walking and maybe we'll run into someone you know."

They walked until evening then laid down to rest.

Morning came and they were weak from hunger. With all the birds around, Hodi decided to go catch breakfast. She remembered everything her mother had taught her.

There were also plenty of insects for a hungry tarantula to feast on. They walked a long, long time toward the mountain until dark. The wind began to blow stronger and stronger.

Hodi began her journey up the mountain. It had gotten very cold and she was exhausted. She fell down to rest. Uhuru explained that he could no longer continue because he did not have the fur of lions. He would have to walk back to the desert.

"No, I need you," Hodi said.

"No you don't. You'll be fine. Besides, the desert is where I belong. Please, go without me, but promise me you'll always remember and honor our friendship."

"I promise," Hodi reluctantly agreed to part.

Uhuru walked back toward the desert and Hodi walked up the mountain until evening. The morning finally arrived. Hodi woke up rubbing her eyes and yawning. "Whoa, it's cold," she said with her teeth chattering. As she rubbed her eyes, she noticed that her paws were not quite brown anymore. Everything around her was white. She couldn't see anything but white everywhere. "Aaaayyy!! What is this?" She stood up and shook off the fallen snow. "This is so strange."

She rolled around in it. She jumped through piles of it. She leaped from one pile to the next. Then, she heard a giggle.

"Who's there?" Hodi asked.

"Hee, hee. You're funny looking. I've never seen one of you before. How do you do? I'm Adija, a snow goose."

"I'm Hodi, a lion. What do you mean you've never seen one of me before? I'm a big 'ol tough lion don't you know and I eat birds."

"Well, you don't look very big or tough to me and you wouldn't want to eat me," Adija laughed.

"I wouldn't? Why not?"

"I think you're confused. I'm not a bird. I'm a goose, silly."

"I think you're the one who's confused but you might come in handy anyway. What do you do around here for fun?"

"Well pretty much the same thing you were just doing a minute ago. What are you doing here?" Adija asked.

"I'm on an adventure. I came to see what this place is like."

"Come on. I'll show you around, then. We call this Mount Kilimanjaro."

Adija took Hodi around the mountain and showed her all of the fun hills to slide down. She showed her all of the snow caves, and introduced her to her friends.

Hodi began to get cold and tired.

"I think it's time for me to return home now. I have a long way to walk you know. I think I'd better rest in a warm place."

Adija agreed. "Okay, you're right, but you have to take something back to show your family that you were here."

Hodi agreed.

"I have just the thing." Adija smashed snow into snowballs with her feathers. "Put these in your pockets. Don't take them out until you get home so that you don't lose them."

Hodi thanked her and started running down the mountain toward the desert. After running awhile, she started to feel dizzy and saw two of everything. She was almost out of the cold and back into the desert but she just couldn't go any farther. She fell down to rest. While she was resting, a butterfly came and landed on her nose.

It called in a beautiful voice, "Hodi....."

She opened her eyes and managed to shake the snow from her head. The butterfly fell off of her nose and landed in the snow.

It called, "Hodi, wake up. You have to leave this place right now."

Hodi sat up and fixed her eyes on this creature. She saw the butterfly and it looked exactly like the one that had landed on her nose when she was hunting. It was so bright and beautiful.

She replied, "I want to go home, but I need to rest."

"You can't rest here. It's not safe for you. Just walk a little farther. When you get to the warmth of the desert, you can rest there for only a little while."

Hodi stood to her feet and started to follow the butterfly from the bitter cold of the mountain climate. She checked her pockets and the snow was still safely tucked away.

She made it into the warm desert by evening and her almost frozen body started to unthaw. The butterfly flew away. Hodi laid down to rest safely. When morning came, she started her walk toward home. She walked and walked and walked. It felt like days. One evening, to her delight, she could see the forest from afar. She decided to rest for the night and walk all day through the forest to avoid another encounter with Ferny and Lucy. She couldn't remember her path exactly. Hodi walked for a long time through the forest. She couldn't wait to get home to show everyone her treasure. Finally, she found the grassland but it seemed unusually still and quiet. There were no lions or other animals busying about. She found her family under a tree. There were Father Lion, Mother Lion, Mimi Leopard and Juma Leopard fast asleep.

She proudly exclaimed, "Hey everybody, it's me! I'm back and I have something to show you!" No one moved. She went and shook her father. "It's me, Hodi." Father Lion opened one eye and said, "Hi, Hodi. I'm so glad to see you."

"I have something to give you. What's the matter with you all?"

Her mother said, "We are all so hungry, Hodi. There's a drought and many of the animals have moved away."

"I know a place where we can go. I saw it on my journey and I found this too!" She remembered the snow in her pocket. Then, she pulled out a paw full of nothing but water.

She was horrified to see that the snow had melted. "What happened to my snowballs?"

Mother lion comforted Hodi, "I don't know what a snowball is but this water is just what we need. You have to show us to this place."

"Well, I can't take you to the mountain but I can take you to a river. I saw it on my way."

Father lion embraced her. "You're my daughter. You have made me so proud. I'm glad that you are mine."

"Well father, you may not be proud when we get there. You see, we may not be able to go into the land. There are a couple of lion bullies who have taken over the entire grassland there and they won't let anyone pass."

"Don't worry," Father responded. "We'll bring the whole pride with us and ask politely."

Hodi led the way. When they finally reached the top of the hill overlooking the new found land, Hodi began to shake with fear. She was thinking about her run-in with the two lions.

"Father, what if they don't want to let us through?"

"I suspect that they won't, but if they give us any trouble, then...." He paused and turned to look at the crowd of hungry, thirsty lionesses looking on. Hodi and Father started to drink the water. They heard voices behind them.

"Well, well, well what have we here? Oh, look it's the little coward that we ran off before. Did you bring us some more munchies? Ha, ha, ha," the bullies taunted the two.

Father Lion said, "We have traveled here because we are in need of a new home. Our land has dried up and we just want to pass through this land."

"Save it pops! We own this place and we aren't sharing it with anybody. Now beat it!"

They growled and lunged at Father and Hodi. The pack of lionesses and leopards at the top of the hill rushed down and surrounded the two on every side. The two bullies quickly backed off and made what sounded like a meow. They ran away deep into the grassland.

All the pride recognized Hodi as a heroine. They immediately organized the territory. They were all happy and well fed. From time to time, Hodi sees that beautiful butterfly and is reminded of her experience at the mountain called Kilimanjaro.

CPSIA information can be obtained at www.ICGtesting.com
Printed in the USA
BVIW12n0134080115
382260BV00001B/1